The Fawn Gloves

By

Jerome K Jerome

British Library Cataloguing-in-Publication Data
A catalogue record for this book is available from the
British Library

Jerome K. Jerome

Jerome Klapka Jerome was born in Walsall, England in 1859. Both his parents died while he was in his early teens, and he was forced to quit school to support himself. Jerome worked for a number of years collecting coal along railway tracks, before trying his hand at acting, journalism, teaching and soliciting. At long last, in 1885, he had some success with *On the Stage – and Off,* a comic memoir of his experiences with an acting troupe. Jerome produced a number of essays over the following years, and married in 1888, spending the honeymoon in "a little boat" on the Thames.

In 1889, Jerome published his most successful and best-remembered work, *Three Men in a Boat.* Featuring himself and two of his friends encountering humorous situations while floating down the Thames in a small boat, the book was an instant success, and has never been out of print. In fact, its popularity was such that the number of registered Thames boats went up fifty percent in the year following its publication. With the financial security provided by *Three Men in a Boat,* Jerome was able to dedicate himself fully to writing, producing eleven more novels and a number of anthologies of short fiction.

In 1926, Jerome published his autobiography, *My Life and Times*. He died a year later, aged 68.

Always he remembered her as he saw her first: the little spiritual face, the little brown shoes pointed downwards, their toes just touching the ground; the little fawn gloves folded upon her lap. He was not conscious of having noticed her with any particular attention: a plainly dressed, childish-looking figure alone on a seat between him and the setting sun. Even had he felt curious his shyness would have prevented his deliberately running the risk of meeting her eyes. Yet immediately he had passed her he saw her again, quite clearly: the pale oval face, the brown shoes, and, between them, the little fawn gloves folded one over the other. All down the Broad Walk and across Primrose Hill, he saw her silhouetted against the sinking sun. At least that much of her: the wistful face and the trim brown shoes and the little folded hands; until the sun went down behind the high chimneys of the brewery beyond Swiss Cottage, and then she faded.

She was there again the next evening, precisely in the same place. Usually he walked home by the Hampstead Road. Only occasionally, when the beauty of the evening tempted him, would he take the longer way by Regent Street and through the Park. But so often it made him feel sad, the quiet Park, forcing upon him the sense of his own loneliness.

He would walk down merely as far as the Great Vase, so he arranged with himself. If she were not there--it was not likely that she would be--he would turn back into Albany Street. The newsvendors' shops with their display of the cheaper illustrated papers, the second-hand furniture dealers with their faded engravings and old prints, would give him something to look at, to take away his thoughts from himself. But seeing her in the distance, almost the moment he had entered the gate, it came to him how disappointed he would have been had the seat in front of the red tulip bed been vacant. A little away from her he paused, turning to look at the flowers. He thought that, waiting his opportunity, he might be able to steal a glance at her undetected. Once for a moment he did so, but venturing a second time their eyes met, or he fancied they did, and blushing furiously he hurried past. But again she came with him, or, rather, preceded him. On each empty seat between him and the sinking sun he saw her quite plainly: the pale oval face and the brown shoes, and, between them, the fawn gloves folded one upon the other.

Only this evening, about the small, sensitive mouth there seemed to be hovering just the faintest suggestion of a timid smile. And this time she lingered with him past Queen's Crescent and the Malden Road, till he turned into Carlton Street. It was dark in the passage, and he had to grope his way up the stairs, but with his hand on the door of the bed-sitting room on the third floor he felt less afraid of the solitude that would rise to meet him.

All day long in the dingy back office in Abingdon Street, Westminster, where from ten to six each day he sat copying briefs and petitions, he thought over what he would say to her; tactful beginnings by means of which he would slide into conversation with her. Up Portland Place he would rehearse them to himself. But at Cambridge Gate, when the little fawn gloves came in view, the words would run away, to join him again maybe at the gate into the Chester Road, leaving him meanwhile to pass her with stiff, hurried steps and eyes fixed straight in front of him. And so it might have continued, but that one evening she was no longer at her usual seat. A crowd of noisy children swarmed over it, and suddenly it seemed to him as if the trees and flowers had all turned drab. A terror gnawed at his heart, and he hurried on, more for the need of movement than with any definite object. And just beyond a bed of geraniums that had hidden his view she was seated on a chair, and stopping with a jerk absolutely in front of her, he said, quite angrily:

"Oh! there you are!"

Which was not a bit the speech with which he had intended to introduce himself, but served his purpose just as well--perhaps better.

She did not resent his words or the tone.

"It was the children," she explained. "They wanted to play; so I thought I would come on a little farther."

Upon which, as a matter of course, he took the chair beside her, and it did not occur to either of them that they had not known one another since the beginning, when between St. John's Wood and Albany Street God planted a garden.

Each evening they would linger there, listening to the pleading passion of the blackbird's note, the thrush's call to joy and hope. He loved her gentle ways. From the bold challenges, the sly glances of invitation flashed upon him in the street or from some neighbouring table in the cheap luncheon room he had always shrunk confused and awkward. Her shyness gave him confidence. It was she who was half afraid, whose eyes would fall beneath his gaze, who would tremble at his touch, giving him the delights of manly dominion, of tender authority. It was he who insisted on the aristocratic seclusion afforded by the private chair; who, with the careless indifference of a man to whom pennies were unimportant, would pay for them both. Once on his way through Piccadilly Circus he had paused by the fountain to glance at a great basket of lilies of the valley, struck suddenly by the thought how strangely their little pale petals seemed suggestive of her.

"'Ere y' are, honey. Her favourite flower!" cried the girl, with a grin, holding a bunch towards him.

"How much?" he had asked, vainly trying to keep the blood from rushing to his face.

The girl paused a moment, a coarse, kindly creature.

"Sixpence," she demanded; and he bought them. She had meant to ask him a shilling, and knew he would have paid it. "Same as silly fool!" she called herself as she pocketed the money.

He gave them to her with a fine lordly air, and watched her while she pinned them to her blouse, and a squirrel halting in the middle of the walk watched her also with his head on one side, wondering what was the good of them that she should store them with so much care. She did not thank him in words, but there were tears in her eyes when she turned her face to his, and one of the little fawn gloves stole out and sought his hand. He took it in both his, and would have held it, but she withdrew it almost hurriedly.

They appealed to him, her gloves, in spite of their being old and much mended; and he was glad they were of kid. Had they been of cotton, such as girls of her class usually wore, the thought of pressing his lips to them would have put his teeth on edge. He loved the little brown shoes, that must have been expensive when new, for they still kept their shape. And the fringe of dainty petticoat, always so spotless and with never a tear, and the neat, plain stockings that showed below the closely fitting frock. So often he had noticed girls, showily, extravagantly dressed, but with red bare hands and sloppy shoes. Handsome girls, some of them, attractive enough if you were not of a finicking nature, to whom the little accessories are almost of more importance than the whole.

He loved her voice, so different from the strident tones that every now and then, as some couple, laughing and talking, passed them, would fall upon him almost like a blow; her quick, graceful movements that always brought back to his memory the vision of hill and stream. In her little brown shoes and gloves and the frock which was also of a shade of brown though darker, she was strangely suggestive to him of a fawn. The gentle look, the swift, soft movements that have taken place before they are seen; the haunting suggestion of fear never quite conquered, as if the little nervous limbs were always ready for sudden flight. He called her that one day. Neither of them had ever thought to ask one another's names; it did not seem to matter.

"My little brown fawn," he had whispered, "I am always expecting you to suddenly dig your little heels into the ground and spring away"; and she had laughed and drawn a little closer to him. And even that was just the movement of a fawn. He had known them, creeping near to them upon the hill-sides when he was a child.

There was much in common between them, so they found. Though he could claim a few distant relatives scattered about the North, they were both, for all practical purposes, alone in the world. To her, also, home meant a bed-sitting room--"over there," as she indicated with a wave of the little fawn glove embracing the north-west district generally; and he did not press her for any more precise address.

It was easy enough for him to picture it: the mean, close-smelling street somewhere in the neighbourhood of Lisson Grove, or farther on towards the Harrow Road. Always he preferred to say good-bye to her at some point in the Outer Circle, with its peaceful vista of fine trees and stately houses, watching her little fawn-like figure fading away into the twilight.

No friend or relative had she ever known, except the pale, girlish-looking mother who had died soon after they had come to London. The elderly landlady had let her stay on, helping in the work of the house; and when even this last refuge had failed her, well-meaning folk had interested themselves and secured her employment. It was light and fairly well paid, but there were objections to it, so he gathered, more from her halting silences than from what she said. She had tried for a time to find something else, but it was so difficult without help or resources. There was nothing really to complain about it, except-- And then she paused with a sudden clasp of the gloved hands, and, seeing the troubled look in her eyes, he had changed the conversation.

It did not matter; he would take her away from it. It was very sweet to him, the thought of putting a protective arm about this little fragile creature whose weakness gave him strength. He was not always going to be a clerk in an office. He was going to write poetry, books, plays. Already he had earned a little. He told her of his hopes, and her great faith in him gave him new courage. One evening, finding a seat where few people ever passed, he read to her. And she had understood. All unconsciously she laughed in the right places, and when his own voice trembled, and he found it difficult to continue for the lump in his own throat, glancing at her he saw the tears were in her eyes. It was the first time he had tasted sympathy.

And so spring grew to summer. And then one evening a great thing happened. He could not make out at first what it was about her: some little added fragrance that made itself oddly felt, while she herself seemed to be conscious of increased dignity. It was not until he took her hand to say good-bye that he discovered it. There was something different about the feel of her, and, looking down at the little hand that lay in his, he found the reason. She had on a pair of new gloves. They were still of the same fawn colour, but so smooth and soft and cool. They fitted closely without a wrinkle, displaying the slightness and the gracefulness of the hands beneath. The twilight had almost faded, and, save for the broad back of a disappearing policeman, they had the Outer Circle to themselves; and, the sudden impulse coming to him, he dropped on one knee, as they do in plays and story books and sometimes elsewhere, and pressed the little fawn gloves to his lips in a long, passionate kiss. The sound of approaching footsteps made him rise hurriedly. She did not move, but her whole body was trembling, and in her eyes was a look that was almost of fear. The approaching footsteps came nearer, but a bend of the road still screened them. Swiftly and in silence she put her arms about his neck and kissed him. It was a strange, cold kiss, but almost fierce, and then without a word she turned and walked away; and he watched her to the corner of Hanover Gate, but she did not look back.

It was almost as if it had raised a barrier between them, that kiss. The next evening she came to meet him with a smile as usual, but in her eyes was still that odd suggestion of lurking fear; and when, seated beside her, he put his hand on hers it seemed to him she shrank away from him. It was an unconscious movement. It brought back to him that haunting memory of hill and stream when some soft- eyed fawn, strayed from her fellows, would let him approach quite close to her, and then, when he put out his hand to caress her, would start away with a swift, quivering movement.

"Do you always wear gloves?" he asked her one evening a little later.

"Yes," she answered, speaking low; "when I'm out of doors."

"But this is not out of doors," he had pleaded. "We have come into the garden. Won't you take them off?"

She had looked at him from under bent brows, as if trying to read him. She did not answer him then. But on the way out, on the last seat close to the gate, she had sat down, motioning him to sit beside her. Quietly she unbuttoned the fawn gloves; drew each one off and laid them aside. And then, for the first time, he saw her hands.

Had he looked at her, seen the faint hope die out, the mute agony in the quiet eyes watching him, he would have tried to hide the disgust, the physical repulsion that showed itself so plainly in his face, in the involuntary movement with which he drew away from her. They were small and shapely with rounded curves, but raw and seared as with hot irons, with a growth of red, angry-coloured warts, and the nails all worn away.

"I ought to have shown them to you before," she said simply as she drew the gloves on again. "It was silly of me. I ought to have known."

He tried to comfort her, but his phrases came meaningless and halting.

It was the work, she explained as they walked on. It made your hands like that after a time. If only she could have got out of it earlier! But now! It was no good worrying about it now.

They parted near to the Hanover Gate, but to-night he did not stand watching her as he had always done till she waved a last good-bye to him just before disappearing; so whether she turned or not he never knew.

He did not go to meet her the next evening. A dozen times his footsteps led him unconsciously almost to the gate. Then he would hurry away again, pace the mean streets, jostling stupidly against the passers-by. The pale, sweet face, the little nymph-like figure, the little brown shoes kept calling to him. If only there would pass away the horror of those hands! All the artist in him shuddered at the memory of them. Always he had imagined them under the neat, smooth gloves as fitting in with all the rest of her, dreaming of the time when he would hold them in his own, caressing them, kissing them. Would it be possible to forget them, to reconcile oneself to them? He must think--must get away from these crowded streets where faces seemed to grin at him. He remembered that Parliament had just risen, that work was slack in the office. He would ask that he might take his holiday now--the next day. And they had agreed.

He packed a few things into a knapsack. From the voices of the hills and streams he would find counsel.

He took no count of his wanderings. One evening at a lonely inn he met a young doctor. The innkeeper's wife was expecting to be taken with child that night, and the doctor was waiting downstairs till summoned. While they were talking, the idea came to him. Why had he not thought of it? Overcoming his shyness, he put his questions. What work would it be that would cause such injuries? He described them, seeing them before him in the shadows of the dimly lighted room, those poor, pitiful little hands.

Oh! a dozen things might account for it--the doctor's voice sounded callous--the handling of flax, even of linen under certain conditions. Chemicals entered so much nowadays into all sorts of processes and preparations. All this new photography, cheap colour printing, dyeing and cleaning, metal work. Might all be avoided by providing rubber gloves. It ought to be made compulsory. The doctor seemed inclined to hold forth. He interrupted him.

But could it be cured? Was there any hope?

Cured? Hope? Of course it could be cured. It was only local--the effect being confined to the hands proved that. A poisoned condition of the skin aggravated by general poverty of blood. Take her away from it; let her have plenty of fresh air and careful diet, using some such simple ointment or another as any local man, seeing them, would prescribe; and in three or four months they would recover.

He could hardly stay to thank the young doctor. He wanted to get away by himself, to shout, to wave his arms, to leap. Had it been possible he would have returned that very night. He cursed himself for the fancifulness that had prevented his inquiring her address. He could have sent a telegram. Rising at dawn, for he had not attempted to sleep, he walked the ten miles to the nearest railway station, and waited for the train. All day long it seemed to creep with him through the endless country. But London came at last.

It was still the afternoon, but he did not care to go to his room. Leaving his knapsack at the station, he made his way to Westminster. He wanted all things to be unchanged, so that between this evening and their parting it might seem as if there had merely passed an ugly dream; and timing himself, he reached the park just at their usual hour.

He waited till the gates were closed, but she did not come. All day long at the back of his mind had been that fear, but he had driven it away. She was ill, just a headache, or merely tired.

And the next evening he told himself the same. He dared not whisper to himself anything else. And each succeeding evening again. He never remembered how many. For a time he would sit watching the path by which she had always come; and when the hour was long past he would rise and walk towards the gate, look east and west, and then return. One evening he stopped one of the park-keepers and questioned him. Yes, the man remembered her quite well: the young lady with the fawn gloves. She had come once or twice--maybe oftener, the park-keeper could not be sure--and had waited. No, there had been nothing to show that she was in any way upset. She had just sat there for a time, now and then walking a little way and then coming back again, until the closing hour, and then she had gone. He left his address with the park-keeper. The man promised to let him know if he ever saw her there again.

Sometimes, instead of the park, he would haunt the mean streets about Lisson Grove and far beyond the other side of the Edgware Road, pacing them till night fell. But he never found her.

He wondered, beating against the bars of his poverty, if money would have helped him. But the grim, endless city, hiding its million secrets, seemed to mock the thought. A few pounds he had scraped together he spent in advertisements; but he expected no response, and none came. It was not likely she would see them.

And so after a time the park, and even the streets round about it, became hateful to him; and he moved away to another part of London, hoping to forget. But he never quite succeeded. Always it would come back to him when he was not thinking: the broad, quiet walk with its prim trees and gay beds of flowers. And always he would see her seated there, framed by the fading light. At least, that much of her: the little spiritual face, and the brown shoes pointing downwards, and between them the little fawn gloves folded upon her lap.

-THE END-